# Marvin and the BOOK of MAGIC

# Marvin and the BOOK of MAGIC

## JENNY PEARSON

Illustrated by
**Aleksei Bitskoff**

Barrington Stoke

Published by Barrington Stoke
An imprint of HarperCollins*Publishers*
Westerhill Road, Bishopbriggs, Glasgow, G64 2QT

www.barringtonstoke.co.uk

HarperCollins*Publishers*
Macken House, 39/40 Mayor Street Upper,
Dublin 1, DO1 C9W8, Ireland

First published in 2024

Text © 2024 Jenny Pearson
Illustrations © 2024 Aleksei Bitskoff
Cover design © 2024 Ali Ardington

ISBN 978-1-80090-269-5

10 9 8 7 6 5 4 3 2 1

A catalogue record for this book is available from the British Library

Printed at Pureprint, a Carbon Neutral® printer

This book contains FSC™ certified paper and other controlled
sources to ensure responsible forest management.

For more information visit: www.harpercollins.co.uk/green

*For Angus Todd Morton Batman –*
*keep making your own magic*

# CONTENTS

# CHAPTER 1

## Never Trust a Squirrel

My name is Marvellous Marvin. You might have heard about me from the show *TV's Most Talented Kids*. Well, from the bloopers if you didn't catch it live – they had 4.2 million views when I last looked. Yup, I'm *that* kid – the one who went on TV to perform magic tricks and ended up destroying the entire set.

Frankly, I blame the squirrel. I'd *thought* it might be more exciting to pull a bushy-tailed rodent from a hat instead of the standard white rabbit. I thought it would really impress the celebrity judges. But here's a lesson for you – never trust a squirrel.

Squirrels are not as well behaved as rabbits, I discovered. It was just after I'd announced my name on stage. The little blighter leaped out from the secret box I had him in and attacked me. Bit me right on the nose.

My natural reaction was to get the squirrel off me. So I grabbed him and chucked him. He flew off, his little ears flapping, towards the left of the stage.

The squirrel landed, rather expertly, on one of the legs of the stilt walker who was waiting in the wings. And then he started to scramble up the stilt.

The stilt walker did not respond to this calmly. She started running about on her long wooden limbs in a right panic. She screamed. A lot. Then she wobbled as she tried to kick the squirrel off. Of course, stilt-girl lost her balance.

As she fell, she grabbed hold of a rope. The rope stopped stilt-girl from hitting the floor. But it also pulled down one of the ceiling lights.

Right on top of the piano.

The piano was smashed to pieces – which did not please the kid who was going to be playing Beethoven's Fifth Symphony on it with his feet. He stomped onto the stage and started yelling. Unluckily for him, he'd been eating a peanut bar just moments before. The squirrel must have caught a whiff of peanut because he jumped off stilt-girl and landed on piano-boy's head.

Piano-boy started running around in circles and then ran straight into a large water tank. It had been standing ready to be wheeled to the centre of the stage. The tank was supposed to be for an act called Tracey Turtle. Apparently, Tracey had trained some turtles to do a dance routine in the water.

Let's just say, the turtles did not get to dance that day.

The tank wobbled backwards and forwards. Then it seemed to stay frozen on its edge for a moment. Before finally tipping over. On top of the judges.

They gave me three loud buzzers. And a lifetime ban from ever applying to appear on the show again.

Anyway, of course I'd told everybody I knew that I was going to be on TV. So everybody I knew saw what had happened. As you can imagine, I was a laughing stock at school.

My dad has always been very encouraging of my magical efforts and told me not to worry about it. He said that people would forget. And then Dad fell about laughing. Again.

It turns out that people forget a lot of things – to do their homework, where they left their phone, to brush their teeth (maybe that's just me). But they do not forget about the time a kid with a squirrel made a celebrity judge cry on TV because a tankful of water ruined his hairdo.

Anyway, I gave up magic after that. I couldn't face doing it again. All I'd ever wanted to be was a magician, but that dream was over.

See, my grandad was a magician – and a great one. I'll never forget the first time he sawed my nanna in two at one of my birthday parties. Grandad Jim always wanted to entertain me. He was pretty much my favourite person.

Before he died, Grandad Jim told me that I had the family gift for magic. The gift had skipped my dad and gone straight to me. Unlucky, Daddy-o! Knowing this had made me feel special. And I practised magic every day.

Grandad Jim got sick and couldn't get out of the house, so I'd go round to see him. I saw it as my turn to entertain him. I'd try out some of my new tricks, and he'd give me tips and encouragement. Dad said it was the only time Grandad Jim really seemed like himself those days.

But then Grandad Jim died. And after the TV show disaster, I decided he'd been wrong about me having the gift. I'd pretty much made up my mind that I'd never do magic again. But then something happened. Something truly magical. And everything changed.

# CHAPTER 2

## Me and Magic Are Done

It was a few months after my TV disaster. I was still hearing the odd shout of, "Watch out, Marvin, there's a squirrel!" as I walked around school. It was mostly Ryan and Herman. Two kids in my class who wouldn't let me forget it.

Along with shouting at me, they'd put peanuts in my locker, and once they even attached a fake fluffy squirrel tail to my bag. I walked around with the tail all morning before I noticed. But the teasing wasn't happening every single second – which it had felt like in the weeks right after the show.

I was walking to lunch with my friend Asha. We came across Miss Tilney stapling a poster onto a noticeboard. She stuck the staple gun into her utility belt filled with school stationery and said, "I do hope you will both sign up."

"School talent show!" Asha read out. "Hey, Marvin, this could be your big comeback!"

Asha was about the only person who hadn't made fun of me. She thought my act had been the best thing she'd ever seen on TV.

I groaned and said, "I told you. Me and magic are done."

"You could just do something that doesn't involve a live animal," Asha said. "You could show Ryan and Herman that you are actually a really talented magician!"

"No," I said. "I'm not performing ever again."

"Suit yourself," Asha said. "I'm going to sign up."

"What are you going to do?" I asked.

"I think I'll sing," she replied.

"Sing?" I said. I tried to sound encouraging. But I'm afraid to say, Asha has a truly dreadful singing voice.

"Yeah, sing and maybe dance and maybe paint something."

It seemed that Asha had decided to choose the three things she was worst at: singing, dancing and art.

"Wow," I said. "All at the same time?"

Asha rolled her eyes. "*Obviously*. Anyone can do just one of those – that would hardly be showing talent."

I had been joking when I'd said all at the same time. But maybe Asha was on to something. Maybe doing three truly terrible acts together would be something spectacular.

"I think you'll be brilliant," I said. "What are you going to sing?"

"Maybe 'Bohemian Rhapsody' so I can do all the voices too."

"I cannot wait!" I said.

"I know I'm not the best at those things," Asha continued as we headed off to lunch. "But I think that what I lack in ability I can make up for in enthusiasm."

"You definitely are not short of enthusiasm," I told her.

*

Dad must have read the parent email about the talent show because he brought up the subject over tea that evening.

He dolloped some baked beans onto my plate. "I think you should give this talent show a go, Marvin," Dad said.

"Nope," I told him. "I'm not making a fool of myself."

"You won't! You'll be great!" Dad dropped two hotdogs from a tin onto the beans.

"I am not standing up in front of a room full of people ever again. Especially if that room includes Ryan and Herman."

"They still giving you a hard time?" Dad asked. "Want me to email your teacher?"

I shrugged. "I can handle it."

Dad nodded, then pushed his beans around his plate with his fork. "Your grandad thought you had talent," he said.

"Well, he was wrong," I replied.

"It's your decision. But listen, kid. You can't let one knock stop you from doing what you love. Things go wrong sometimes, and you have to pick yourself up and try again."

"Why do I have to?" I asked.

"Because that's what people do."

"You don't."

"What do you mean?" Dad said.

"You've given up on heaps of stuff."

"Like what?"

"Like your last diet," I said. "The gym. That time you started Italian lessons because you liked that woman from your work. You don't do any of those any more—"

"Yes, all right, I get the picture," Dad interrupted. "I just think it's a shame that's all. It makes me sad to see your box of tricks sitting there doing nothing. Why don't you get out your cards, or do that thing you do with the colourful hankies? Or maybe use those cups to make my five-pound note disappear? Actually, maybe not that. You've magicked away a lot of cash from me over the years!"

"No, I just can't," I told him. "I'm going to take all my magic stuff to that shop in town. The weird-looking one that buys all sorts of odd things."

"Clive's Emporium?" Dad said. "The one with the stuffed marmoset in the window?"

"Is that what that is? Yeah, there."

"They're your things, but I think it's a shame."

"I think it's necessary," I said. Being honest, it hurt too much to look at them. They sat in my room doing nothing, reminding me that I was letting Grandad Jim down. And how wrong he had been about me.

# CHAPTER 3

## Clive's Emporium

That Saturday, I carried my box of tricks the mile into town and pushed open the door of Clive's Emporium. A little bell tinkled above my head. I'd never been inside before, but I had often stopped to look at the weird and wonderful things displayed in the window.

That day, there was a steel drum and a glass box containing a long snakeskin. An old sewing machine and a spinning wheel. A picture of King Charles painted with the face of a dog. Probably a King Charles spaniel, I realised.

There was a large urn that had "Doreen 1882–2012" engraved on it. I imagined it didn't actually contain Doreen as that would have made her 130. I don't think people last that long. There was also a pirate's hat, a wooden leg and an empty bird cage. Oh, and the stuffed marmoset.

I couldn't imagine what sort of people would buy any of those things. Clive's shop wouldn't be my first choice for Christmas-present shopping.

I was so busy taking it all in that I hadn't noticed Clive pop up behind the counter.

"Greetings," he said loudly.

I turned round to see a man wearing a white fake-fur coat. Under the coat, he wore a flowery Hawaiian shirt and a velvet tie. He had dark eyebrows but a neatly trimmed white beard.

"Hi," I said, mouth open.

"How can I help you today?" Clive said. "Did something in my window capture your heart?"

I was about to say *absolutely not*, but he added, "No, I see you have an offering for me! How delightful!"

Clive stepped around the counter. For some reason it wasn't a surprise to see he was wearing a kilt on his bottom half.

"Now, darling child, what have you there?" Clive asked.

"It's my box of magic tricks," I said.

He threw his hands in the air and said loudly, "How wonderful, a magician in my shop! Yes, I see it now!"

"See what?" I said.

"You have the gift of magic in you!" Clive replied.

"I really don't. I want to get rid of all this stuff."

He stalked over to me and started to rummage about in the box. "Yes, yes," he said. "I think you should leave these with me."

"Good," I said.

"For these do not contain real magic!"

"No," I said. "They're just tricks."

"Certainly not of a standard for someone with your gift," Clive added.

I was beginning to realise that Clive might be someone who wasn't always in touch with reality. "How much will you give me for it all?" I said, trying to get to the real business.

"Thirty pounds, OR ..." Clive said that *OR* very loudly.

"Or?" I said.

"Or I can give you something else in exchange."

To be honest, I really wanted the cash, but I was also curious about what else Clive might offer.

He started rummaging around in the shop, moving skeletons and bagpipes and a unicycle out of the way. Then Clive stopped and said a triumphant, "A-HA!"

"An old book?" I said. The book he was holding was small and had two gold Ms embossed on the dark brown leather. "It's a tempting offer, but I think I'll take the cash."

"Don't be so hasty," Clive said. "This isn't any old book. This is a *magic* book."

Obviously, I didn't believe him. Would you take the word of a man named Clive wearing a fake-fur coat and kilt?

"Your face tells me you don't believe me!" Clive said.

"It's not that I don't believe you," I said. "It's just I'm not sure that what you're saying is exactly true."

"This book," Clive said, waving it in the air, "will show those with the gift of magic how to use it."

"I don't have the gift of magic," I said.

"Ah, but you've been told you have before! I can tell! Who was it?"

I frowned. "My Grandad Jim," I said.

"Your Grandad Jim?" Clive paused and tilted his head. "Yes, Grandad Jim is a magical-sounding name."

"*Is it?*" I said.

"Your Grandad Jim saw the magic in you, Marvin.  He believed in you."

At this point I was 99 per cent certain Clive was trying to trick me into handing my magic box over for a worthless old book instead of taking the cash.  But there was 1 per cent of me that thought, *What if it's true?  What if Grandad Jim was right?*

And it was this 1 per cent that made me say, "I'll take the book."

Clive beamed.  "A wise choice!"

I popped my box on the counter, and he handed over the book and did a little bow.

"Goodbye, Marvin," Clive said.

I walked towards the door, the small leather-bound book in my hand.  I was already getting a strong feeling that I'd just been conned.  Then a thought struck me.

I turned round and asked, "Hey, how did you know my name?"

But Clive had vanished.

# CHAPTER 4

## An Accidental Badger

When I got home, Dad was watching the football. His team, the Blackburn Badgers, were playing. I didn't fancy watching, so I went upstairs and sat down on my bed.

I pulled the book out of my back pocket to take a closer look. On the front were the letters MM.

"Marvellous Marvin?" I said. The letters couldn't really stand for that. It had to be a coincidence.

I opened it and turned to the first page.

In swirly writing it said:

# Book of Magic

"Original title," I joked.

I watched, astonished, as some words appeared.  As if by ... well, magic.

*All right, smarty pants, you come up with something better.*

I gave my eyes a rub.  I had to have imagined it.  But there were the words, as clear as day.

"This is one weird book," I said.  The words disappeared and new ones formed.

*Who are you calling weird, squirrel boy?*

"Hey!" I said. "How are you doing that?"

*The clue's in the title.*

"Magic?"

*Well, duh.*

My mind was reeling. "So you really are a magic book?" I said.

*Bet you're glad you didn't take the thirty quid now, hey?*

"Too right! And you can teach me to do real magic?"

*I can show you how to do the magic of real magicians. Not silly wizardy magic. But the magic of showmen! Whether you can do it is another thing.*

"I've got a school talent show next week," I said. "Do you think you can teach me by then?"

*A school talent show? Are you kidding me? Not exactly the Big Time, is it?*

"I've seen the Big Time and didn't like it," I replied, thinking about the TV show. "I just want everyone who knows me to stop thinking I'm such a loser."

*That sounds challenging.*

"Hey!"

*Sorry, carry on.*

"I want to do the magic show to end all magic shows!" I told the book. "I want to make the head teacher disappear. I want to walk through walls. I want to ... I don't know ... pull badgers out of my armpits!"

*Excuse me?*

"Sorry, I don't know why I said that badger thing. Think it was because Dad's Blackburn

Badgers team is playing.  Anyway, I was just getting a bit carried away."

*You can do the badger thing if you want.*

"No, I've learned not to mix animals and magic."

*Wise.  So, what do you want to start with?*

"Could you show me how to make myself disappear?"

*Certainly.  First you must bend your arms at the elbows and move them up and down.*

"OK," I said.  "I'm doing that."

*Now jut your head forward and back.*

"I'm jutting!"

*Finally, say, "I am a chicken."*

30

I stopped flapping and jutting. "Hey!" I complained.

*Everyone always falls for that.*

"Very funny," I said, feeling a bit silly that I'd been tricked by a book. Even if it was a magic one. "Can you be serious now?"

*Yes, sorry. Place your hand on my page. Then imagine yourself vanishing into nothing.*

"That's it?" I said.

*You have to really believe it can happen or it won't work.*

"I believe it can happen," I said, and put my hand on the book. I closed my eyes and imagined myself turning into nothing. Which is actually a lot harder to do than you might think. And for some reason I thought of a badger again.

I'm sure you can work out what happened.

Yup. I turned myself into a badger.

A tingling sensation spread across my body. The next thing I knew, there was a poof of smoke, and I was looking at two furry paws.

It wasn't the best timing for my dad to open the door.

He clearly has a fear of badgers, despite supporting the footballing version, because Dad screamed and shut the door again.

"Marvin!" Dad shouted. "Where are you? There's a badger on your bed!"

I quickly put my hand back on the book and imagined myself back as me.

Luckily, I had fully transformed by the time Dad opened the door again.

"I ..." Dad began. "I could have sworn there was a ..." He looked around, puzzled.

"Could have sworn what?" I asked innocently.

Dad shook his head. "Never mind. I came up to tell you that Asha's mum just texted. Asha's on her way over."

"OK, great," I said.

Dad looked around the room again, then closed the door.

I looked down at the book.

*Well, that's never happened before. Maybe we should start with something simpler.*

"Yeah, maybe we should," I said.

# CHAPTER 5

## The Incredible Talents of Asha

Asha bounded into my room and flumped down onto my bed. She started speaking before I could tell her anything about the book. "Listen, I've been practising my act all morning. Do you think it is too much of a stretch to paint the *Mona Lisa* in the time it takes me to sing 'Bohemian Rhapsody'?"

It was an odd question. But the sort of thing I'd come to expect from Asha. "Errr. How long is the song?" I asked.

"Five minutes and fifty-five seconds."

The thought of listening to Asha sing for nearly six minutes did not fill me with joy. But she was my friend, and I wanted to be supportive. "It will be a challenge," I said. "You might not recreate it perfectly, but I'm sure you will give it your best shot."

"That's what I thought," Asha said. "Hey, do you want to see what I've practised so far?"

"Absolutely. But how are you going to paint and dance at the same time?"

"I'll just dab at the canvas when I'm near it," Asha explained. "I've tried to include more lower-body dance moves."

"Like an Irish dancer?" I asked.

"A bit. Mostly when the music gets fast. I'll show you."

Asha put the song on her phone and started singing along. If you haven't heard

"Bohemian Rhapsody", you should take a listen. My dad says it's a classic.

It started off very slowly. Asha warbled along to the lyrics, swaying about and whipping her arms around to the gentle voices.

"Right now," she said, "when it's going slow, I'll be able to get lots of the painting done. With long strokes like this."

"Yes, I see," I said.

"How do I look?"

The real answer was, "A bit like an over-excited octopus", but I said, "Very elegant."

Asha carried on singing. Badly. All the while she was also pretending to paint an invisible canvas. She swayed during the entire ballad section – her movements getting bigger and bigger. Then she stopped still and clutched her hand to her chest during the operatic part, I think to portray the emotion.

She really started going for it when the hard-rock section began and the music properly kicked off. Her legs waggled about in all directions underneath her, her head banging up and down in a frenzy. Asha did a bit of air guitar, some air drums and some other air instruments that I would not be able to name. Then, when it was finally over, she fell onto my bed panting.

Asha looked up at me, eyes wide. "So, what did you think?"

I said, "I have never seen anything quite so incredible in all my life." Which was the truth.

"Thank you," she said, beaming.

"Asha," I said. "I've been thinking. I might actually do the talent show after all."

She bolted upright. "Really? That's brilliant, Marvin!"

"See, the thing is, I *can* do magic," I said.

"I know you can! You have found my right card every single time you do the trick!"

"No, I mean I can do actual magic! I've got a book!" I held up the book.

"Looks old," Asha said.

"It's a magic book."

"Cool. Does it teach you how to do tricks?"

"No, it shows me how to do actual magic," I said.

"Actual magic? No way! Like what?"

I lowered my voice. "Earlier, I turned myself into a badger."

"A badger? Why would you want to do that?" Asha asked.

"I was trying to make myself vanish. But I thought about a badger instead."

Asha put her hand on my forehead. "Are you feeling OK?"

"I feel great! Look, I'll show you."

I opened up the book and put my hand on the page. This time I thought about vanishing. Disappearing into nothing. An absence of me. The tingles spread across my body. I started to feel light. Was it working? Was I vanishing?

Asha suddenly gave a massive gasp. "Oh my days! Marvin! Where did you go?"

# CHAPTER 6

## Too Much Floating

"I'm right here!" I said.

Asha's head swivelled about like an owl. "Where?" she asked.

I prodded her arm. "Here!"

She jumped back. "Oh, my actual days! You made yourself disappear!"

"I know," I said.

"Can you change back?"

"Yeah." I put my invisible hand back on the book. That was harder to do than I expected. Turns out that not being able to see a body part makes it hard to direct said body part accurately. Somehow, I managed to slap myself in the face.

Anyway, I managed to get my hand on the book in the end and imagined myself back as me.

43

I reappeared in a satisfying poof of smoke.

Asha looked at me wide-eyed. "That. Was. Amazing! One moment you were here – the next gone!" She picked up the book and looked it over. "This is an ACTUAL MAGIC BOOK!"

I grinned. "Uh-huh."

"Where did you get it from?" Asha asked.

"Clive's Emporium!"

"I love it there! I'm saving up to buy that painting of the King Dog! How does the book work?"

"It's really cool," I said. "I talk to it, and it writes back to me."

"Shut up! It does not!"

"Want to see?"

"Errr, does a pigeon have a tongue?" Asha said.

"I don't think they do."

Asha frowned. "Really? Anyway, yes! I want to see!"

"OK, watch this." I opened the book and said, "Hello, *Book of Magic*, it's me, Marvin."

Asha gasped when the writing appeared.

*I know it's you, Marvin. And your friend is right. Pigeons do have tongues. They are called piston tongues and act a bit like straws. This means pigeons can drink without having to tilt their heads back.*

"Wow! That is one smart book!" Asha said. "Now get it to do some magic."

"What would you like to see?" I asked.

Asha's forehead crumpled, her eyes looked from left to right and she stuck her tongue out. This is Asha's thinking face. I see it every day at school – whenever Miss Tilney asks her a question.

"I know!" Asha suddenly shouted. "Can you make me levitate?"

"*Book of Magic*, can you help me to make Asha levitate?"

*Place one hand on my pages and one in the sky. Then imagine your friend rising up.*

Asha lay down on the carpet. "Get on with it then," she said. "Make me float in mid-air!"

I put one hand on the book. I raised the other in the air and thought about Asha floating up towards the ceiling.

"Ooooh! I feel all tingly!" she said. And then she began to rise upwards.

"It's HAPPENING! I'm floating!" Asha yelled.

Asha was floating. Upwards and upwards. Until she slammed face-first into the ceiling.

"Too much floating! Too much floating!" she said. "You're squashing me with your magic, Marvin!"

I tried to imagine Asha floating softly to the ground like a feather. But instead, I imagined her dropping much faster. The image that came to mind was actually that of a cannonball.

Asha landed on the carpet with a bit of a thud.

"I'm OK!" she said, leaping up almost immediately. "That was the coolest thing ever! I was like some haunted girl from a horror movie!"

"It was pretty mind-blowing," I said.

"You have an actual magic book, Marvin! Think of the fun we could have with this at school! Oh my days! You are totally going to win the talent show. It'll beat my act hands down!"

I suddenly felt a bit bad. Asha had worked really hard on her act. Sure, it was a bit strange, but it was all her. I started to wonder if I'd be cheating by using the book.

"I think your act is very unique," I said. "The judges might love your ... creativity."

"There is always a chance," Asha said. "I might have to up my game and add in a pogo-stick."

I didn't know what to say to that, so I changed the subject. "Shall we try something else?"

"Go on then!" Asha said. "Maybe you could magic us up a bar of chocolate the size of a human. I'm getting a bit hungry."

"Now *that* sounds like a good idea!" I picked up the book. "*Book of Magic*, can you show me how to magic up a bar of chocolate the size of me?"

*Oh, I'm sorry. You've used up your three magic tricks.*

# CHAPTER 7

## Everything Comes in Threes

"What do you mean, I've used up my three magic tricks?" I asked the *Book of Magic*.

*You get three chances to use the magic.*

"You never said anything about me only having three chances!"

*Did I not? Whoopsie.*

"Whoopsie?" I said. "Is that all you can say?"

*You never asked. You were so keen to get going. Besides, surely you know that is how these things work. It's only ever three chances.*

Asha nodded to agree. "It's got you there, Marvin," she said. "Three is a standard number. It's the number of wishes genies grant. It's what good things come in. It's also the number of men in a boat ..."

"Yes, I get the picture—" I said.

"Peanut-butter cups come in threes. There are three blind mice ..." Asha went on.

"OK, I get it!" I said. "Threes! I just think the book might have warned me!" I sat down on the bed and put my head in my hands. "This is an actual disaster. I've wasted the magic!"

"I don't think you can say you wasted it," Asha said.

I gave her a look. "I turned myself into a badger, disappeared and squashed you into the ceiling! How is that not wasting the magic?"

"It was fun at the time?" Asha said uncertainly.

"But I was going to prove to Ryan and Herman, to everybody, that I was a real magician. A great magician. Now I'm always going be the squirrel kid."

Asha put her hand on my arm. "Marvin," she said. "If it makes you feel better, from now on I shall think of you as the badger kid."

I had to laugh at that. Then I sighed. "I should have known I'd mess it up. I always mess things up. I guess I hoped that if I was this amazing magician, Grandad Jim might be looking down on me. Then he'd know he was right about me having the gift of magic. He might be proud."

Asha looked at me with pity in her eyes. The pity quickly turned into something much angrier. Luckily, I realised her anger was directed at the book and not at me.

She picked it up and waved it about. "Did you hear that, *Book of Magic*?" Asha said.

*The bit where he was feeling sorry for himself? Some of it. To be honest, I switched off at the end. No one enjoys listening to a moaner.*

"Oi! I wasn't moaning," I said. "I was having a moment of reflection!"

*Sounded like moaning to me.*

"Look, there must be something you can do. Surely there must be a way you can give Marvin one more magic trick?" Asha said.

*I'm afraid it is out of my control.*

Asha put a hand on her hip. "In that case," she said, "I would like to speak to your manager."

"I don't think that will work," I said.

She cupped her hand by her mouth. I think it was so the book wouldn't hear. "You watch. My mum does this sort of thing all the time."

*My manager?*

"Yes, your manager," Asha said. "And don't tell me you don't have one. *Everyone* has someone they answer to. Now, I'm guessing there is something in your job description that states you have to explain the terms and conditions to any new consumer. And I'm also guessing that your manager would be very interested to hear that this did not happen."

Asha and I stared at the page, waiting for a response.

I'd just about given up hope when some
writing appeared.

*I do not think we need to bother my*
*manager with this. I can grant you one more*
*magic trick.*

"Great!" I said, but Asha slapped her hand
over my mouth.

She leaned in to me and whispered, "Never accept the first offer." Then she cleared her throat. "That is a start, but I think we would also like that chocolate bar we mentioned. So that's two magic tricks."

*Deal.*

"Excellent," Asha said.

*Place your hand on the book and think of your chocolate then.*

I know it was only writing, but I read it as if it was written in a very snotty tone.

I put my hand on the book and imagined a chocolate bar as big as me. There was a poof of smoke. When it cleared, I was facing a chocolate version of me.

"Choc-o-tastic!" Asha said. "Bagsy your ears!"

"Why do you want my ears?" I asked.

"Why do you think?  They're massive!"
Asha said.

# CHAPTER 8

## A Plan for Something Spectacular

Asha and I sat cross-legged on my carpet and managed to eat from my head down to my elbows. It turns out that not even we could finish my whole body's worth of chocolate.

"Thinking about it now," Asha said, licking her fingers, "I should have probably asked the book for two new magic tricks instead of one and the chocolate."

I stopped munching and swallowed. "Let's not think about that now."

"At least you've got one magic trick left for the talent show," Asha said. "What do you think you're going to do?"

"I'm not sure yet, but I want it to be really spectacular."

Asha let out a big chocolatey burp. "Naturally. Oooh, maybe you should set yourself on fire!"

"I think that might be too alarming for the younger years," I said.

"That is an excellent point," Asha agreed. "Maybe we should ask the book what the best-ever magic trick is?"

"Could try, I suppose." I picked up the magic book and opened the cover. *"Book of Magic?"*

*Oh, hello, gluttons. I thought you had forgotten about me.*

"Sorry," I said. "Excellent chocolate by the way. We have a question for you."

*Do tell. The suspense is killing me.*

I could tell the book was being sarcastic, but I decided to rise above it. "What is the most spectacular magic trick I could do?"

*Depends who you ask.*

"We're asking you," I said.

*In that case, walking on water always goes down well. People talked about the last guy who did that for years.*

"I don't think we can get a swimming pool in the school hall. What else have you got?"

*You could saw yourself in half?*

"You know, I don't really fancy that," I said.

*What about the vanishing trick? You managed that without too much trouble.*

"Yeah, I did, didn't I? I could vanish on stage. Then run to the back of the hall and reappear!"

"That would be sooooo cool!" Asha said. "Ryan and Herman will vomit with jealousy!"

"OK, so that's it solved!" I said. "I'm going to do Marvellous Marvin's Vanishing Trick at the school talent show!"

"And you are going to be spectacular!" Asha said.  Then she jumped up.

"Where are you going?" I asked.

"Better get home to practise on my pogo-stick, hadn't I?  You, badger boy, have upped the game!"

Asha skipped off down the stairs, her hair bunches bobbling about behind her.

I picked up the book.  "So, *Book of Magic*, what shall we talk about?" I said.

*How nice silence is?*

"Ha, good one.  Maybe I could ask you about magic?"

*If you must.*

"Where does it come from?" I asked.

*Magic is everywhere. It's as big as the universe and yet so small it can live inside a single cell.*

"Does everyone have magic in them?"

*Yes, but not many know it is there. And even then, most are not able to use it to become a real magician. You are one of a very few.*

I liked the thought of that! "Are there more books like you?" I said.

*There are. But I wouldn't say the others are as skilled as me. I have worked with many of the greats.*

"What is the one thing you have learned from all the magicians you've worked with?"

*That just because you can use magic to help you, it doesn't mean you should.*

# CHAPTER 9

## Show Time

The school talent show was after school on Wednesday. On Monday and Tuesday, I kept the *Book of Magic* wedged down the back of my waistband. I was terrified I was going to lose it and ruin my big comeback.

Thanks to Asha, word had got round that my act was going to be really amazing.

Ryan and Herman cornered me in the corridor on Wednesday lunch-time. "Anyone smell peanuts?" they asked.

"Yeah, ha, very good," I said as I tried to get past them.

"We hear this act of yours is supposed to be really something," Ryan said.

I shrugged and said, "Guess we'll see."

"Yeah, guess we shall," Herman said, looming over me.

"Got any fluffy-tailed animals in this one?" Ryan said.

"Nope," I said.

"Sounds boring to me," Herman said.

Asha bowled over at that point, her pogo-stick in hand. "It is not boring," she said. "It is super amazing, and it is going to blow your tiny minds!"

Then she grabbed me by the arm, and we walked into registration together.

I couldn't concentrate during afternoon lessons. It wasn't because I was nervous. I was impatient. I couldn't wait to show Ryan and Herman how spectacular I could be and wipe the smirks off their faces.

Finally, after I'd struggled through History and Science, the clock hands turned to three thirty. It was time.

I carried Asha's easel and paints while she bounced along beside me on her pogo-stick.

We got to the school hall.  All the kids were sitting on the floor, and all the parents were sitting at the back on fold-down seats.  There were twenty-four acts in total, starting with the Year Ones and ending with the Year Sixes. Asha was the second-last person to perform. I was the very last.

"That's because everyone knows you're going to be the grand finale!" Asha whispered to me as we took our seats backstage.

I touched the back of my trousers to check the book was still there.  It was.

It took ages for all the acts to perform.  Let's just say the standard was not what I would call professional.

We watched a Year One juggle with one ball. So it wasn't really juggling.  Just more throwing and catching. Or not catching in the case of that Year One.

A couple of Year Twos recited a poem about bumble bees. To be fair, they were pretty cute.

Some Year Threes did some drama where they played three witches. It was from the play *Macbeth*, apparently, and pretty terrifying. Once they'd finished, it was a whole thirty seconds before the stunned audience realised they should clap.

It was after this performance that Dad poked his head round the backstage curtain.

"Pssst. Marvin, over here!" Dad said.

I ran over to him. "Dad, you can't be back here. It's for performers only."

"I won't be long," he said. "I just wanted to wish you good luck. And to tell you I'm proud

of you.  Oh, and I also wanted to give you this.
I thought you might need it."

He pushed my box of tricks past the curtain.

"You bought them back from the shop?" I said. "Thanks, that's so kind. But I've moved on from those tricks."

"Well, take them anyway. You never know."

I took the box from him. "I'd better go back."

"OK," Dad said. "Good luck. I'm sure Grandad Jim is looking down on you right now."

"That's a nice thought," I said.

I sat down next to Asha and watched the final Year Five performers. There were a lot of musicians – a recorder player, a violinist, a saxophone player. All differing levels of terrible.

And then it was Asha's turn. I helped her carry her easel onto the stage. I showed the audience the blank canvas. Steadied her when she climbed onto her pogo-stick. And finally, I handed her the paint palette and brush.

"Good luck," I said, and hurried away to watch her from the wings.

The spotlight shone on Asha, and she gave a massive smile. "Hello, my name is Asha James, and today I will be painting the *Mona Lisa* whilst singing 'Bohemian Rhapsody' and pogoing. I hope you enjoy it."

# CHAPTER 10

## A Pogo Stick, a Painting and My Very Own Magic

After Asha announced her act, there were a few mutters and murmurs of "She's doing *what*?" from the audience. I felt my stomach flip with nerves for her. The music started to play, and Asha started to sing and bounce and wave her arms around dramatically.

I felt a huge surge of emotion. Asha knew she wasn't going to win, but she was happy to go out there and do her best all the same. Sure, her best was more than a little bit unusual, but as I watched her, I realised how truly amazing Asha was. She was singing all the right notes, just not in the right order. But she didn't care. She was bouncing faster and faster as the music picked up tempo. She was enjoying herself, and there was something magical about that.

I watched, eyes wide, as she slopped paint on the canvas. I knew immediately that there was no way the end product was going to look anything like the *Mona Lisa*. But Asha's enthusiasm seemed to be winning the audience over. Everyone was smiling. True, they also looked confused, but they were loving it!

But then I spotted them. Ryan and Herman sitting in the back row. They were laughing and pointing. Making fun of her. Filming her on their phones. They were probably going to put it on the internet. Then the whole world would laugh at her. Like they had laughed at me.

I couldn't let that happen. Not to Asha. Asha who had always been there for me! I knew I had to do something. But what? Straight away, I knew the answer.

I whipped out the magic book and opened it.

"*Book of Magic*," I said, "I want to make Asha's painting look exactly like the *Mona Lisa*."

*Good for you, Marvin, good for you. Place your hand on my pages and imagine the portrait.*

I closed my eyes and imagined the *Mona Lisa*. I opened them again as the music was fading out and Asha jumped down off her pogo-stick.

She looked at the painting. Blinked once. Blinked again. Rubbed her eyes. Then she leaned in closer. Then her jaw dropped down to her ankles. Slowly, Asha turned the canvas round and said, "Oh my actual days! It never turned out this well in practice!"

The audience gasped one great big gasp. Everyone in the hall looked stunned. Which was understandable. People started to point at

the painting. They were nudging each other and saying things like, "Do you see that? That's incredible! The likeness!"

Then suddenly one man shouted, "The girl is a genius!"

And the whole room erupted into applause. Everybody was on their feet – clapping and whooping.

Asha bowed and curtsied and then did the worm on the floor to celebrate. Then finally she waved and made her way off stage.

I gave her a massive hug. "Now *that* was spectacular!" I said.

"It was, wasn't it?" Asha said. "I can't believe it! I'm sorry, Marvin, but I think I've given you a bit of competition there."

"You certainly have," I said. "Right, wish me luck!"

"Good luck," she said. "Show everyone what you can do."

"Thanks," I said. "I'm going to try my best."

I put the book back in my waistband, picked up my box of magic tricks and walked out on stage.

I took a deep breath. I hoped I looked confident, but my whole body was nervous. "My name's Marvellous Marvin," I began. "Today, I'm going to perform a magic trick. Don't worry, no squirrels will be involved." I got a laugh for that. "It's my favourite one. Someone very special taught it to me. I wish he was around to see it. But who knows? Maybe he is." I suddenly felt a little overwhelmed thinking of Grandad Jim. But then I saw my dad giving me a thumbs up, and it made me feel better.

I took a step forward. "Now, could I have a couple of volunteers?" I asked.

I scanned the crowd, but I knew who I was going to choose. "Ryan and Herman, can you come on down?"

Ryan and Herman did not look like they wanted to *come on down*. But Miss Tilney looked at them very sternly, and they shuffled their way towards me.

"Now, Herman," I said, "could you do me a favour and stand at the far end of the stage?"

Herman shrugged and went and stood where I told him.

"Ryan, you come over and stand with me," I added.

Ryan walked over, and I held out a pack of cards. "Ryan, pick a card, any card."

Ryan grabbed a card from the middle of the pack.

"Show the audience your card," I said. "Good, now put it back in the pack."

I shuffled the cards so they streamed between my hands, which got me a round of applause. I picked out a card and held it up. "Ryan, is this your card?" I asked.

"No!" he said, clearly delighted I'd got it wrong.

"Oh dear. Err, how about this one?" I said, selecting another card.

"Nope!" Ryan replied.

I could see the audience shifting in their seats. I tried again. "Maybe this one?"

"Not that one either," Ryan said. "You really are a rubbish magician, Marvin."

"Oh dear. Errr ..." I said.

The audience started to mutter. I could see that they were finding it uncomfortable to watch.

"Herman," I called over to him. "Could you do me a favour?"

"Go on."

"Put your hand in your pocket," I told him. "Is there anything in there?"

Herman put his hand in his pocket and pulled out a card. He frowned. "Hey, that wasn't there before!"

"Could you show it to Ryan?" I said.

Herman held up the card. "Ryan, is that your card?" Herman asked.

Ryan looked from the card to me and back to the card again. He clearly couldn't believe it.

"That is my card!" Ryan said. "Herman, that's my card! He only went and found my card! That was amazing!"

I hadn't expected such a positive reaction, but Ryan really was astounded. "How did you do that?" he said. "How?!"

"Magic!" I said, and then I turned to the audience and bowed.

When I straightened up, the audience started clapping. It wasn't quite as loud as the applause Asha had got, but then I hadn't painted the *Mona Lisa* whilst jumping on a pogo-stick and singing "Bohemian Rhapsody". But that didn't matter. I had my magic back. My own magic, and I couldn't stop smiling.

I spotted my dad standing up and clapping his hands together with real feeling. I think he may even have had tears in his eyes. The big softy.

When I got backstage, Asha flung her arms around me and gave me a big hug before I could say anything.

"That was brilliant, Marvin!" Asha said. "You really showed them what you can do! But why didn't you use the *Book of Magic*?"

"Someone once told me that just because you can use magic to help you, it doesn't mean you should."

Asha scrunched up her nose. "That someone has clearly never magicked up a person-sized bar of chocolate."

I laughed. "Yeah, possibly."

"Where did you learn that trick?" Asha asked. "It was so good! Did you see Ryan's face when Herman pulled out his card? *That* was a moment, I tell you!"

"My Grandad Jim taught me. He was the best."

"Well, he'd be really proud of you today," Asha said.

"I hope so," I said. "And you know what, I'm proud of me too. I did the right thing."

"You did great. I'm pleased for you. But can we please remember that *I* was the one who painted an identical copy of the *Mona Lisa* whilst singing 'Bohemian Rhapsody' and bouncing on a pogo-stick?"

"Asha, I don't think I will ever be able to forget that," I said.

She grabbed me by the hand. "Come on, Marvellous Marvin, they're going to announce the winners."

When I got home that evening, I put my third-place trophy on the mantlepiece. Asha had won, obviously, but the scary Year Three witches had taken second place. Dad complained the whole way home that I'd been robbed, but it didn't bother me. I'd done my best, and that was all that mattered.

Dad ordered a pizza delivery for tea because he said we were celebrating me finding my magic again. He passed me a slice and said, "You know, I have a magic trick?"

"You do?" I said.

"Yes, watch me make this pizza disappear!" Dad said, and folded an entire slice into his mouth.

"Very impressive," I said.

"Not as impressive as you, kid. I was so proud of you today. But then, I always am."

It was only when I was getting changed for bed that I remembered the book. I wanted to say thank you. But when I reached for it in my waistband, it had vanished.

Just like magic.

Our books are tested
for children and young people by
children and young people.

Thanks to everyone who consulted on
a manuscript for their time and effort in
helping us to make our books better
for our readers.